Pinkalicious

and the New Teacher

by Victoria Kann

HARPER FESTIVAL
An Imprint of HarperCollinsPublishers

P9-CWD-549

With love and gratitude to our teachers
—V.K.

The author gratefully acknowledges the
artistic and editorial contributions of
Robert Masheris and Kamilla Benko.

HarperFestival is an imprint of HarperCollins Publishers.

Pinkalicious and the New Teacher
Copyright © 2014 by Victoria Kann
PINKALICIOUS and all related logos and characters are trademarks of Victoria Kann
Used with permission.
Based on the HarperCollins book *Pinkalicious*
written by Victoria Kann and Elizabeth Kann, illustrated by Victoria Kann
For information address HarperCollins Children's Books,
a division of HarperCollins Publishers, 195 Broadway, New York, NY 10007
www.harpercollinschildrens.com

Library of Congress catalog card number: 2013943883
ISBN 978-0-06-218913-4

Book design by Kirsten Berger
14 15 16 17 18   LEO   10 9 8 7 6 5 4 3 2
❖
First Edition

It was the first day of school, and I couldn't wait to show my friends my new sparkly boots and pinkatastic lunch box. I was so excited about my new pink accessories, I forgot something else would be brand new. . . .

Ms. Penny

"Welcome! My name is Ms. Penny," said my new teacher. "Please find your name on the table and take a seat."

Welcome back, students!

Rose

Alison

I looked for my seat. It was all the way across the room from my best friend, Alison.

"Last year, we got to choose where to sit," I told Ms. Penny.

Ms. Penny smiled and said, "New seats, new people to meet."

My chair was in the corner. I hate the corner.

MONTHS OF THE YEAR

January	July
February	August
March	September
April	October
May	November
June	December

It had started to rain, so we had indoor recess. Alison and I drew a pinknificent palace on the chalkboard.

"Splendid, Princess Alison!" I said. "However, it's not a castle without a royal unicorn in a royal garden."

"True, your Royal Pinkness," said Alison. "Shall we plant pink roses or pink peonies?"
"Both!" I told her.

"Look how happy your unicorn looks in the sunny garden you drew!" Ms. Penny exclaimed.

Ms. Penny might be okay after all.

Count by 2:   2   4   6   8

Count by 5:   5   10   15   2(

Count b   10   20   30

After lunch, we went back to the classroom. I couldn't believe my eyes. The pink palace and unicorn were gone! Our masterpieces had been erased.

Ms. Penny isn't okay at all—I wanted my old teacher back!

"It's story time!" Ms. Penny announced later that afternoon. I looked around.

"Ms. Penny, it can't be story time!" I said. "Last year, we always had story time on the comfy, shaggy reading rug."

"I'm sorry, Pinkalicious, but I don't have a shaggy reading rug. I do have beanbag chairs, though. They're not shaggy, but they are comfy."

Reading is PINKATASTIC!

Reading is
PINKATASTIC!

I'm a
pinkatastic
reader!

I read a
PINKALICIOUS
book today!

I read a
PINKALICIOUS
book today!

For more Pinkalicious fun visit
ThinkPinkalicious.com

HARPER FESTIVAL
An imprint of HarperCollinsPublishers
www.harpercollinschildrens.com
Pinkalicious ® and ® Victoria Kann

Reading is Pinkatastic!

Reading is PINKATASTIC!

Reading is PINKATASTIC!

Reading is PINKATASTIC!

I ♥ reading!

I ♥ reading!

I ♥ reading!

I ♥ reading!

"It's not the same."

"Try it. I have a story I think you're going to like."

I wiggled in the crinkly beanbag chair as Ms. Penny read about a girl named Pinkalina who was as big as a pinky finger.

After story time, Ms. Penny told us to write about our summer adventures. My old teacher used to draw smiley faces on our papers. Ms. Penny gave me a star sticker. I liked the star, but I missed getting a smiley face.

This summer I went to the seashore with my family.

name: Pinkalicious

I crossed my arms, slumped in my chair, and scowled at the table.

"Pinkalicious, is everything okay?" Ms. Penny asked.

"I miss sitting next to Alison, and I miss the reading rug and getting smiley faces on my class work."

"The day hasn't been all bad. I saw you laugh during *Pinkalina*. I'm sorry I erased your pictures, but I needed the board for class."

I sighed. "I just miss last year."

"Is there something that your old teacher used to do that we might be able to do this year?"

I thought. Then I got an idea—a PINKERRIFIC idea.

"Pinkalicious told me that your previous teacher used to decorate the classroom," Ms. Penny said. "Any suggestions on how we should beautify the room this year?"

"Let's draw animals and make the room look like a jungle," Rose said.

"What if we draw dinosaurs?" Alex suggested.
I raised my hand. "I know!" I said. "Let's draw ourselves!"
The entire class loved my idea.

Ms. Penny taped paper to the wall and handed out markers. We took turns outlining each other, then decorated the life-size portraits of ourselves.

I drew myself as the Princess of Pink. I was glad my masterpiece couldn't be erased. When we were done, the room looked exciting and colorful.

Ms. Penny wasn't so bad. I thought I was going to like my new teacher. In fact, she was pretty pinkamazing.

We all looked at Ms. Penny's portrait. . . .

She was the Queen of Pink!

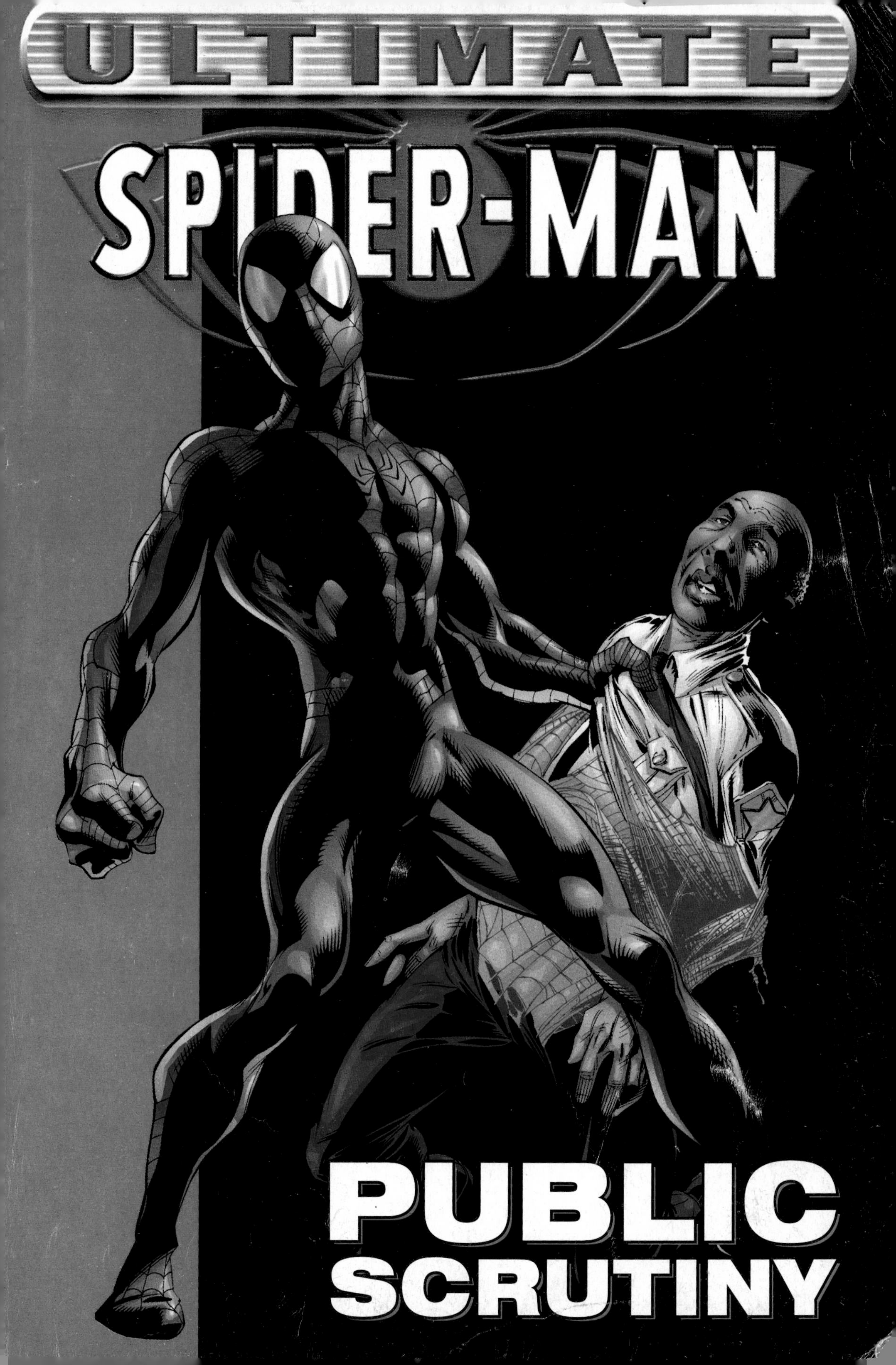
ULTIMATE
SPIDER-MAN
PUBLIC
SCRUTINY

PUBLIC SCRUTINY

script
BRIAN MICHAEL
BENDIS

pencils
MARK BAGLEY

inks
ART THIBERT

colors
TRANSPARENCY
DIGITAL

ULTIMATE SPIDER-MAN VOL. 5: PUBLIC SCRUTINY. Contains material
originally published in magazine form as Ultimate Spider-Man #28-32.
First printing 2003. ISBN# 0-7851-1087-9. Published by MARVEL
COMICS, a division of MARVEL ENTERTAINMENT GROUP, INC. OFFICE
OF PUBLICATION: 10 East 40th Street, New York, NY 10016. Copyright
© 2002 and 2003 Marvel Characters, Inc. All rights reserved. $11.99 per
copy in the U.S. and $19.95 in Canada (GST #R127032852); Canadian
Agreement #40668537. All characters featured in this issue and the
distinctive names and likenesses thereof, and all related indicia are
trademarks of Marvel Characters, Inc. No similarity between any of the
names, characters, persons, and/or institutions in this magazine with
those of any living or dead person or institution is intended, and any
such similarity which may exist is purely coincidental. Printed in
Canada. STAN LEE, Chairman Emeritus. For information regarding
advertising in Marvel Comics or on Marvel.com, please contact Russell
Brown, Executive Vice President, Consumer Products, Promotions and
Media Sales at 212-576-8561 or rbrown@marvel.com

10 9 8 7 6 5 4 3 2 1

letters DAVE SHARPE • associate editor BRIAN SMITH
associate editor C.B. CEBULSKI • editor RALPH MACCHIO

collection editor JENNIFER GRÜNWALD • assistant editors CORY LEVINE & MICHAEL SHORT
associate editor MARK D. BEAZLEY • senior editor, special projects JEFF YOUNGQUIST
senior vice president of sales DAVID GABRIEL
book designer JEOF VITA • vice president of creative TOM MARVELLI
editor in chief JOE QUESADA • publisher DAN BUCKLEY

Well, go get him.

Cover for me-- I'm going to miss fourth period.

It's French-- who cares?

The French.

No kiss?

No time.

AUDIO VISUAL NO JOCKS ALLOWED!

My boyfriend's going to kick your buuuuttt... ♩♪

HYAARRGGHH!!

Everybody back! Back!!

Aunt May?

Hello, sweetie.

What are you doing here?

What are *you* doing here? Why aren't you in class?

I'm-- I have study hall now.

Then why aren't you studying?

Wait, why are you here?

I have a teacher/parent meeting.

You do?

I do.

With who?

With your teacher.

Since when?

I told you about this.

You did not.

I thought I did.

Did I do something wrong?

Did you?

Who is it with?

Peter's math teacher?

Oh, hello, Peter.

Yeah.

Hi.

Uh--
what's going on?

This is fateful, why don't you both come in?

What? No! No, I gotta... uh...

I think it would be very good for all of us to discuss this together.

Come, Peter.

Don't get me wrong, Mrs. Parker, Peter is a teacher's dream student.

His natural cognitive abilities are matched perfectly by his creativity and his healthy attitude.

Not only towards learning but of the classroom environment.

The reason I called you down here, Mrs. Parker, is that, over the semester, I have noticed that Peter seems distracted...

...rather... unfocused.

And though it hasn't affected his studies yet, I thought it was worth talking about before the damage is done.

Peter has the possibility of a free ticket to the college of his choice, and I'd hate to have this "sophomore slump" do anything to jeopardize that.

I thought maybe a dialogue would help figure out why Peter seems so...

Peter?

Hmmmm... what?

Your teacher wants to know why you seem so distracted?

I seem distracted?

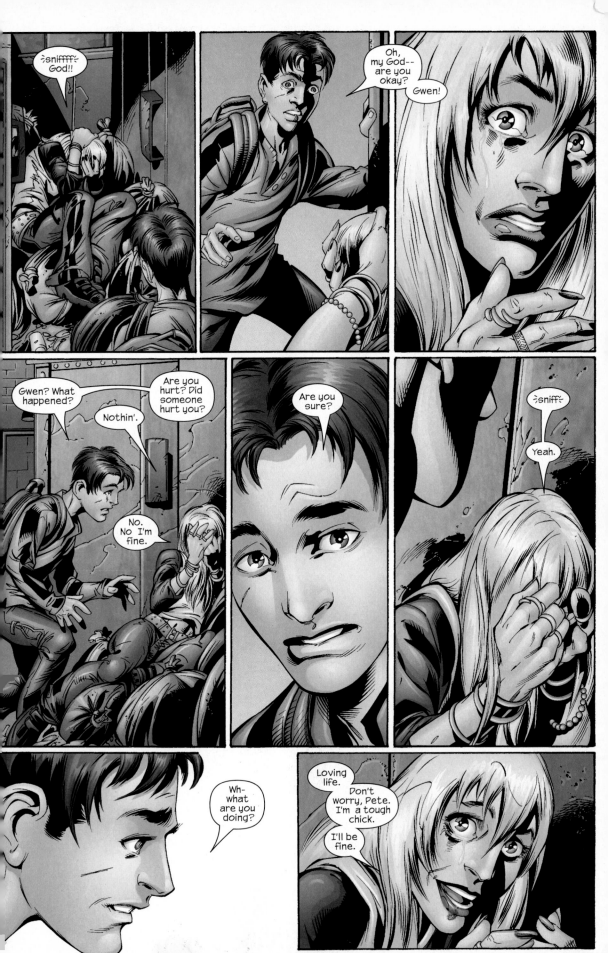

O- okay, then.

Yeah, go ahead!! Everybody else leaves me-- you go too. Go right ahead.

Ooooh GOD!!

Aagghh huhuhuhu nnggggkk!!!

Gwen... ...hey hey hey...

...what's-- what's going on?

I-- I think my Mom is leaving.

My Mom is leaving my Dad and she's leaving me.

I don't think...

I heard her on the phone to one of her idiot friends. I heard her say she hates her life and she's going to leave.

Maybe-- I don't know-- uh-- maybe she was just venting.

You know-- blowing off steam.

Peter?

I know.

You're still here?

I know. I'm trying. This place is like a--

Go! That freak tossed a bus into a Starbucks.

Go to the dumpsters and get Gwen.

What?

Gwen is crying. I left her. I had to. Go and--

She's in a dumpster?

Oh, my God-- I'm coming!

I'm coming!!

Next in line!

Hi. I'm having trouble with my ATM card...

What kind of problem, sir?

It won't give me my money.

Let me see what we can...

Mr. Urich.

(Urich.)

You're not the reporter, Ben Urich?

Yes, I am.

Well, I would shake your hand. You're the guy from the Daily Bugle!

You wrote the piece that took down The Kingpin?

Oh, uh, thanks.

I just wrote a series of articles. The *law* is what took--

You, sir, are a prince.

Oh, well, uh, thank you.

And brave.

Well...

Taking on a man like The Kingpin. Did you win a prize for that or--?

Hey, what do you get paid for something like that?

I'm sorry...

CRASH!

AAAIIEE!

Don't anybody move!!

Oh my God!!

Aunt May!!

Oh my God!!

Oh my God!!

Well, I hate to impose on people--

It's just the way I was raised, I guess, but I really don't know what else I could do.

Put it out of your mind.

Don't give it another thought. She's a great girl and I think--

I know we hardly know each other, but Gwen and I have no other family and-- I promise I would never even dream of--

Well, we single parents have to stick together.

I-- I don't know if I'm cut out to be a single parent.

Oh, please--

I'm scared to death of my own daughter.

And your wife... is officially out of the picture now or--?

Looks like.

I'm sorry-- that was-- that was *rude* of me, wasn't it?

No, no.

Actually, my wife up and *leaving* in the middle of the night without even half an explanation was *rude*.

Poor Gwen... She's so...

She deserves a mother. She deserves better than all this.

Plus-- I am *not* looking forward to being single again-- dating again.

Me either. I am a terrible single person.

Terrible.

SQUEAK

Peter...

Hi...

Hi, sweetie, do you remember Captain Stacy?

Oh, yeah, hello, sir. Hi...

Did you eat? How was work?

No. But uh-- what's going on?

Well, Captain Stacy here has a Police Detectives Conference in Atlantic City this weekend...

...so I offered to let your friend Gwen stay with us until he gets back.

Oh...

Oh?

Yeah, I know.

She's in the house right now?

Yes.

She's sleeping here?

It wasn't my idea.

JUICY 00

Why is she here?

I mean...

JUICY

Her mom up and left... and her dad and my aunt are, I guess, friends now all of a sudden and--

Wait...

...are you angry at me for this?

Hello?

Did you tell her you were Spider-Man?

No!

What are you talking about?

That's-- That's--

You're the only person I told that to.

Well, that was annoying.

Coming up after the break, we talk to a man who knew Captain America way back when and what he thinks of...

What did you answer for number four?

I-- um-- I didn't get to it yet.

I thought MJ was going to study with us?

Yeah, I don't know what happened there...

Um, hold on. Yes. We're going to go live to a situation that is developing uptown.

We have just received word that Spider-Man has been caught in the middle of a jewelry heist on the Upper West Side.

We are going to go live to Shane Jewelers where Monica Kaufman is already on the scene.

Monica? What is the situation down there?

It's a standoff, Dan!

Police have come to the scene here at Shane Jewelers-- where a man that has been identified as the mysterious Spider-Man has trapped himself inside the building...

ABC NEWS
MONICA KAUFMAN

Police have made numerous attempts to negotiate with Spider-Man and there is no word on what the hostage situation is just yet.

But it looks like rumors are true, Spider-Man has officially joined the ranks of criminals.

Aunt May, can I go run over to Mary's for a second?

Aahh!

You remember what I told you...

They'll call the cops. I'm--

You *have* to do this. Just-- just do it.

I'll be here.

Oh my...

Kid! Hey, kid! Can you hear me?

Yo! He just came in here and fell over!

Doctor, he's been shot! One shoulder wound.

Oh, man! The kid's a kid.

There's no ID.

Is he with you?

What? No. No! I'm here with my--

Get him into four or two. Stat!

A and O times four. BP's 132 over 82. Pulse 110.

Number 8 ET tube. What's his BP?

Hold on, pulse OX is low, 82.

Give me four units of O neg, hang two on the rapid infuser.

Doc, lock the ward down and call your security force down here... *now!*

This is E.R. 4. I need as many security guards as you have on duty...

...and call up to Psych and see if they can spare any order--

Hey!! You!!

Yeah, you!!

Hey!

Stop!!

EMERGENCY ROOM

ERGENCY

E.S.

Did-- did you see a girl?

EMS

No...

Was she hot?

Well, Max, a lot of people don't know that I am, in fact, dating Julia Roberts... it's true.

Hahahahahahahahahahaa!!

And it's true, folks. Julia and I have had a secret love child...

Hahahahahahahahahahaa!!

Oh my God...

...Peter...

Drop the guard and put your hands over your head!

I mean it!!!

I'm *not* giving you to the count of three!!

Do it *now*!!!

I was really excited for you this weekend-- "Animal Farm" is about as perfect a piece of writing as was ever created.

It works as both a gripping piece of fiction and as an allegory...

Does anybody know what I mean when I use the word *allegory*?

Anyone?

Peter Parker? Would you like to, maybe, wake up and tell the class what an allegory is?

Uh--

--what?

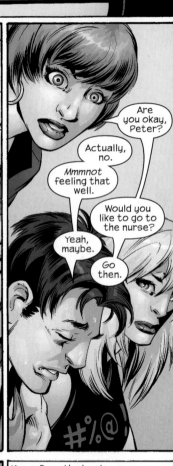

Are you okay, Peter?

Actually, no.

Mmmnot feeling that well.

Would you like to go to the nurse?

Yeah, maybe.

Go then.

Can I take him?

He's a big boy, Mary Jane.

I'm not feeling well either, can I go to the nurse?

Kong, from the book, name me one of the Seven Commandments that the animals painted in big white letters on the barn.

Uh-- what? Animals painting? What kind of book is this?

Oh, man... what am I doing?

I could be *dying* for all I know.

I mean, I got shot last night. An actual cop shot me in the arm with an actual bullet and here I am in class pretending everything is fine.

I am *insane*.

I need sleep. I need to lie down. I need a doctor.

But if I even tried to stay home sick from school, Aunt May would totally have checked me out and seen the huge bandage on my shoulder...

...and I'm a good song and dance man-- but I don't think I can talk my way out of a gunshot wound.

I can't believe how badly I got my--

Peter Parker

BLACK VAN IN PARKING LOT I'LL TAKE CARE OF THE SHOULDER.

Huh.

Well, my spider-sense isn't tingling or whatever it does when I'm about to get pounced on...

If this is Norman Osborn... I quit!

Peter?

...Yeah?

Hi, my name is Janet Van Dyne...

Nick Fury sent me.

happened with you and the cops.

Tough breaks.

Nick figured you might need a doctor who specialized in genetics-- who made house calls.

Yeah, well, I-- I don't need Nick Fury's *help*.

Yes, you do.

Yeah, I do.

Hey, wait-- wait, you're the-- the--

The Wasp... yeah. Card carrying member of the Ultimates.

Hey, that's not too bad at all.

Healing nicely.

Do you have an increased cellular chemokine interleuken-8 or IL-8?

Uh-- I got bit by a spider.

Do you have increased *healing* factor?

I don't know. But I think so.

I haven't done any molecular research on it because my basement microscope only has 4 DIN objectives and--

I remember those.

Wait, what's that?

This will, hopefully, heal you at an even more accelerated rate.

I...

They discovered a chemical in chickens called cCAF that can increase healing time in humans.

I...

One of the things we've been working on in our free time is a specific genetic cocktail based on a synthesis of the patient's own blood sample and the Chemokines.

So I whipped up an interesting little cocktail from your own, very unique, blood sample.

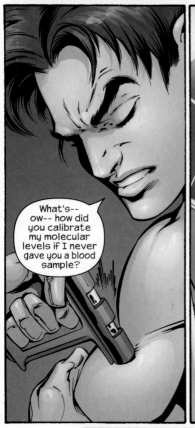

What's-- ow-- how did you calibrate my molecular levels if I never gave you a blood sample?

Look at you, you are smart-- that's cute.

I don't know-- Nick Fury had a blood sample from you.

Consider yourself lucky this happened on TV and that we were watching.

Listen, you may or may not get some flu-like symptoms-- but they'll pass.

Just try to take it easy for a couple of days.

Did Fury happen to mention anything to you about a guy named Harry?

Harry? No.

Fury didn't happen to mention if he knows who that guy is that is running around impersonating me and robbing banks?

No, he didn't say.

And no offense, kiddo, but that kind of thing is small potatoes for us.

But, I tell you, if someone was running around in my costume doing that... I would find him and beat the holy snot out of him.

You know what? You look a million times better than you did in class.

I feel a million times better.

You do?

I really do.

Oh, come on...

What?

Drop the act, man. That was the lamest sick routine I have ever seen.

Eric Roberts laughs at you.

But that's okay, that's nothing prepared to the real *"put on"* you guys are putting on.

Come on, I totally know...

The two of you are sneaking around in the middle of the night...

Dude, you came in at one in the morning.

I heard you.

If my dad caught me out with a guy at one in the morning... he would lock me in a tower like that chick in that movie.

Hey, listen, good for you guys, but you're going to get busted.

Everyone gets busted eventu--

What?

AUNT MAY!

OH NO!

What kind of an idiot tries to rob an armored car at a cop convention?

I mean, think about it!

What did Spider-Man do?

What'd he do? The crumbum makes a run for it!

All the cops got their guns out and this Spider-dude-- he just bolts.

It was just about the scariest thing I ever saw.

All these cops were running and screaming and this Spider-Man guy, he was running across the rooftop of that restaurant over there-- over there-- see? There--

--he was running across the rooftop swearing at the cops in Spanish.

In Spanish?

Yeah, I know.

I always assumed that he was, like, white or something-- but I guess that was pretty racist of me now that I think about it.

And that's when the cops started firing?

Oh, yeah...

So, basically this guy Ben, who is this reporter friend I have at the paper...

...he-- ahem-- he-- he said the same thing those cop friends of your dad said...

...that every one who saw what happened...

...every one of them said he died saving that little boy.

He died a hero.

And-- and I know that doesn't make it any better but-- that's what happened.

They-- uh--

--they don't know what was in the knapsack yet... but they think that it was stuff to open the armored car with-- blow it up or something.

Maybe that plastique stuff-- that playdoh they make bombs with.

Spider-Man...

Don't talk to me-- Urich! Just go!! Go go go!!

Ben, take a photographer with you!

No time, Jonah. Send one down! Meantime, I have my digital.

Call the second you have anything!!

Always do.

Told you, Robbie! Told you!!

Hey, Mr. Robertson...

Oh, hi, Peter, I thought you weren't coming in today...

What's going on?

Oh, that idiot dressing up as Spider-Man got himself into another standoff with the police...

I tell ya, Peter... ...I sincerely hope that this isn't the same Spider-Man and I sincerely hope whoever this reckless maniac is-- I hope they put this guy away for all time.

But you gotta give this moron one thing: when's the last time you've seen an old fashioned, honest-to-goodness, crime spree like this? I mean--

Ooohhhkay...

Too young to be mumbling to myself...

Transparency
Digital

I-I-I--
did it-- I--
it was all
me...

I did
it. I can
prove it and
everything...

Please--
please get
me out of
here...

I promise--
it was me and
me alone-- just-
just... please...

Well, I have an offer.

Peter and I-- we talked about it.

Maybe your mom will come around. I don't know-- I don't know her.

But seeing as I really only know how to cook for three...

...and seeing as we really think the world of you--

--we were hoping that maybe you'd consider staying here.

You know...

...if you want...

How about because I wake up in the middle of the night--

--every night--

--crying!

Did you know that?

I have nightmares, Peter!

Horrible nightmares that you *die!*

You die-- or-- or-- or-- or I die.

Every night!

Do you know that I relive the bridge thing?

I keep reliving the moment-- the exact moment when I was just thrown-- tossed-- off the top of the Queensborough bridge!

Sometimes-- sometimes it happens when I'm awake-- right in the middle of class.

I am sitting in class and-- and-- and I'll start falling.

At first it-- it was cool.

My boyfriend is a super hero.

Oh, my God-- my boyfriend...

But, Peter-- you're going to die doing this.

You're going to die in that stupid costume!

And I know that there is nothing I can say to stop you from doing it.

But I never in a million years imagined that I would be tossed off a bridge by a maniac or-- or-- or wiping your *gunshot blood* off my clothes so my mom doesn't see it

Someone is going to *kill* you.

I-I-I-I can't do this.

※Sniff※

Well, I didn't know that about your dad, did I?

Peter, you never ask!

You never ask about *me*.

It's all about you and and your costume.

And it was fun in the beginning, sure...

How am I supposed to know this about your dad and mom if you don't tell me?

I'm supposed to read your mind?

But for the record--

--its not just Gwen.

It's *all* of it.

I love you, Peter.

I just can't do this.

So, what?

We're done?

HISTORY: NYPD veteran Captain John Stacy's dedication to his job was eroding his family life; his wife Ginger was having an affair while his daughter Gwen grew up a rebellious teen, barely seeing her father due to his police schedule. John was the detective assigned to the Ben Parker murder where he first encountered May and Peter Parker, the victim's wife and nephew. Later, Stacy was called to a factory where Ben Parker's killer was holed up, and glimpsed Spider-Man (secretly Peter Parker) as he delivered the bound criminal to the police.

Gwen began attending Midtown High after being expelled from her last school. While investigating a horrific crime scene where Dr. Octopus had killed a woman, Captain Stacy received a call from the Midtown High principal informing him Gwen had been caught with a knife in school. Meeting reporter Ben Urich outside of the crime scene, Stacy let off some steam; he "thanked" him for cracking the Kingpin case, sending every wannabe gangster in the tri-state area into a power-grabbing frenzy, and asked him why he wasn't chasing sewer monsters. Back at his station, John argued with Gwen, reminding her that if she didn't have a police captain for a father, she would probably be jailed for bringing a weapon into school. Gwen explained that she was sticking up for Peter Parker, who was being bullied at the time, but John was interrupted by a call from Ben Urich before they could finish the conversation. Urich provided John with information about Otto Octavius and his link to the brutal murder, but Gwen ran off during their conversation. John barely managed to get his daughter back into Midtown High, promising the principal there would be no more such incidents.

Ginger finally ran off with another man, abandoning her husband and daughter; with her father at work and nowhere else to go, Gwen turned up at Peter's house in the middle of the night. Peter's Aunt May called John, who came over to collect her, and the two adults bonded. A few days later, with a large detectives' conference in Atlantic City coming up, John asked May if she could watch Gwen for the weekend; May agreed. While there, John witnessed Spider-Man (actually an imposter) robbing an armored car. The false Spider-Man attempted to escape while several officers opened fire on him and a bullet hit his backpack. The imposter tossed the smoking backpack as far as he could, nearly hitting a child. Stacy ran towards the child, pushing him out of the way of the backpack, which he caught. The backpack exploded, killing him. The true Spider-Man later caught the imposter during a bank robbery. With Ginger Stacy unwilling to take responsibility for her child, May Parker offered Gwen a place to stay.

REAL NAME: John Stacy
KNOWN ALIASES: None
IDENTITY: No dual identity
OCCUPATION: Police Captain
CITIZENSHIP: U.S.A.
PLACE OF BIRTH: Unknown
KNOWN RELATIVES: Gwen Stacy (daughter, deceased); Ginger Stacy (wife, separated), unnamed mother
GROUP AFFILIATIONS: NYPD
EDUCATION: College graduate
FIRST APPEARANCE: Ultimate Spider-Man #5 (2001)

HEIGHT: 6'
WEIGHT: 180 lbs.
EYES: Brown
HAIR: Reddish-brown

ABILITIES: John Stacy was a competent and dedicated detective.

POWER GRID	1	2	3	4	5	6	7
INTELLIGENCE							
STRENGTH							
SPEED							
DURABILITY							
ENERGY PROJECTION							
FIGHTING SKILLS							

Art by Mark Bagley